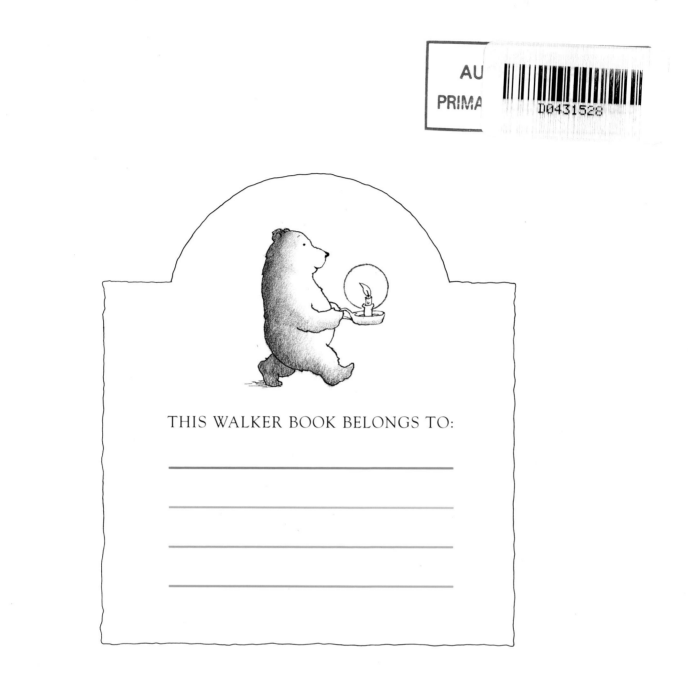

THIS WALKER BOOK BELONGS TO:

_____

_____

_____

_____

TO KIERON, CAIN
& EAMONN PAM PAM

T.C.

TO UNCLE JIMMY

P.A.

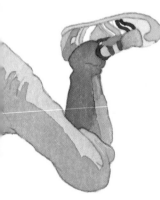

First published 1994 by
Walker Books Ltd
87 Vauxhall Walk
London SE11 5HJ

This edition published 1995

2 4 6 8 10 9 7 5 3

Text © 1994 Trish Cooke
Illustrations © 1994 Patrice Aggs

This book has been typeset in Cochin.

Printed in Hong Kong

British Library Cataloguing in Publication Data
A catalogue record for this book is available
from the British Library.
ISBN 0-7445-4311-8

MR PAM PAM AND THE

HULLABAZOO

Written by
Trish Cooke

Illustrated by
Patrice Aggs

WALKER BOOKS
AND SUBSIDIARIES
LONDON • BOSTON • SYDNEY

Mr Pam Pam comes to my house,

Mr Pam Pam and the baby.

Mr Pam Pam is ever so tall,

his arms and legs are stringy.

He told me his favourite food

is banana ice-cream with gravy.

One day right,
when Mr Pam Pam came to visit,
I was watching telly –
Mum was playing music,
so we didn't hear the door until
Mr Pam Pam lifted the flap
of the letter-box and started
shouting through it:

"PAM PAM KNOCKING
ON YOUR DOOR!"

and Mum went down to open it.

Mr Pam Pam said,
"You'll never believe it
but every word I say is true...

As I was walking round here
to come and see you
I saw a HULLABAZOO,
with yellow hands and
a green moustache!"

Mum laughed.

But me and
Mr Pam Pam's
baby listened.
I've never seen
a Hullabazoo
before.

"And it bounced,
   and it bounced..."
Mr Pam Pam showed us.
"And it twizzled
   and it twizzled
   till it could twizzle
   no more."

"Uh-huh,"
said Mum as she
stood by the door.
"And where is this
Hullabazoo now?"

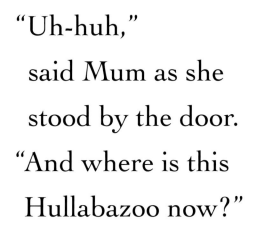

And I rushed to the gate to see it too
because I'd never seen a Hullabazoo.

"Oh, it's gone now," said Mr Pam Pam,
"but it was there when I saw it.
If you'd have hurried up
and opened the door ...
maybe you would
have seen the
Hullabazoo too!"

Mr Pam Pam comes to my house,
Mr Pam Pam and the baby.
Sometimes he takes me to the park,
he lets me push the buggy.
But I can hardly reach the handles
and Mr Pam Pam has to help me.
I like Mr Pam Pam,
Mr Pam Pam and the baby.

One day right,
when I was pushing the buggy,
Mr Pam Pam shouted:

"WELL, GOODNESS GRACIOUS ME!"

I stood on my tiptoes
to try and see
what he could see
but Mr Pam Pam
ran on just a bit ahead
of me and pointed
round the corner.

He said, "You'll never
believe it but every word
I say is true...
As I was walking just
a bit ahead of you
I saw that Hullabazoo,
with yellow hands

and a green moustache.
Its face was covered
in red and black dots
and could you believe
that Hullabazoo
was wearing
purple socks!"

But when I got round
the corner ...
that Hullabazoo
had gone.
I might have seen it
if I'd have run...

Mr Pam Pam comes to my house,
Mr Pam Pam and the baby.
He told me his favourite food
is banana ice-cream with gravy.
So when he came yesterday
Mum made it specially,

but he said, "No, thank you – I've eaten already.

I had dinner with the Hullabazoo.

He's really quite friendly.

You'll like him too."

And in came the Hullabazoo,
with yellow hands and
a green moustache.
Mum laughed.
His face was covered
in red and black dots

and the Hullabazoo
was wearing purple socks,
and a flat orange cap
with a star on the top.

And he bounced

and he twizzled –

A LOT,

A LOT!

And he said:

"I'm a Hullabazoo,
nice to meet you.
I'm a Hullabazoo!"

It's true...

MORE WALKER PAPERBACKS
For You to Enjoy

THE CATS OF TIFFANY STREET
by Sarah Hayes

Every Friday night, six cats meet and dance at the end of Tiffany Street.
Then along comes the man with a van and takes them away.

"Admirably suited to reading aloud … will give great pleasure.
The pictures are bold, colourful and full of movement and witty detail.
The story is a good one too." *The Times Educational Supplement*

0-7445-3162-4   £4.99

EAT UP, GEMMA
by Sarah Hayes / Jan Ormerod

Mischievous baby Gemma drives her family mad when she refuses to eat.

"Great child appeal, accurately reflecting the warmth of family life." *Books for Keeps*

0-7445-1328-6   £4.99

BET YOU CAN'T!
by Penny Dale

"A lively argumentative dialogue – using simple,
repetitive words – between two children. Illustrated with
great humour and realism." *Practical Parenting*

0-7445-1225-5   £3.99